KV-684-637

C29 0000 0782 011

HOW TO MAKE MONEY

FROM
UPCYCLING

RITA STOREY

W

FRANKLIN WATTS

LONDON•SYDNEY

Franklin Watts
First published in Great Britain in 2017 by
The Watts Publishing Group

Copyright © The Watts Publishing Group, 2017

All rights reserved.

Credits
Series editor: Sarah Peutrill
Editor: Sarah Ridley
Packaged by Storeybooks
Series design: Rocket Design (East Anglia) Ltd
Cover design: Peter Scoulding

ISBN 978 1 4451 5282 0

Printed in China

MIX
Paper from
responsible sources
FSC® C104740
FSC
www.fsc.org

Picture acknowledgements
The publisher would like to thank the following for permission to reproduce their photos: Shutterstock/ Amarante Ayo 10; Shutterstock/Rose Carson 19 (bottom); Shutterstock/Andrey Cherkasov 2, 21 (middle); Shutterstock/Denis Cristo 8; Shutterstock/Munkie Dang 16 (bottom right); Shutterstock/elisekurenbina 16 (top right); Shutterstock/Featureflash Photo Agency 29 (bottom); Shutterstock/filborg 14, 16 (left), 19 (top), 21 (top), 22 (top); Shutterstock/graphego 13 (bottom); Shutterstock/N Gvozdeva 11; Shutterstock/Matej Kastelic 5, 17; Shutterstock/NotionPic 15 (top); Shutterstock/Portare fortuna 4 (top), 12, 18 (top); Shutterstock/ Pretty Vectors 23 (top), 32; Shutterstock/robuart 15 (bottom); Shutterstock/Neda Sadreddin 18 (bottom); Shutterstock/siridhata 3 (bottom right), 23 (bottom); Shutterstock/subarashii21 4 (bottom), 6, 7, 9, 22 (bottom), 24, 26, 27, 28, 29 (top); Shutterstock/Elena Vasilchenko 3 (top), 21 (bottom); Shutterstock/UVAconcept 13 (top); Shutterstock vector 3 (bottom left), 25; Shutterstock/Vipavlenkoff 20 (top); Shutterstock/Ria Wonder 20 (bottom); Tudor Photography 15 (middle).

Every attempt has been made to clear copyright. Should there be any inadvertent omission please apply to the publisher for rectification.

Franklin Watts
An imprint of
Hachette Children's Group
Part of The Watts Publishing Group
Carmelite House
50 Victoria Embankment
London EC4Y 0DZ

An Hachette UK Company
www.hachette.co.uk

www.franklinwatts.co.uk

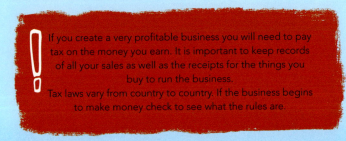

If you create a very profitable business you will need to pay tax on the money you earn. It is important to keep records of all your sales as well as the receipts for the things you buy to run the business.
Tax laws vary from country to country. If the business begins to make money check to see what the rules are.

CONTENTS

Why start a business? 4

Product design 6

The market 8

Marketing 10

Branding 12

Selling on the Internet 14
   Business idea 1: Zap-pow Upcycled comic-strip products

How to sell at a craft fair 16
   Business idea 2: Upsa Dasiy Upcycled garden products

An upcycling blog or vlog 18
   Business idea 3: Lizzie B Craft workshop channel

Production 21
   Business idea 4: Vintage Vogue upcycled costume jewellery

Inventions 22
   Business idea 5: Your very own upcycling invention

People. planet. profit 24

Running your business 26

Setting up a website 27

Now what? 28

Business jargon/Further information 30

Index 32

WHY START A BUSINESS?

Have you ever dreamed of owning your own business?

Does it worry you that we live in a society that throws so much away?

Does running a business appear to be just about making a profit?

Are you worried that starting a business will harm the environment?

If you answer 'yes' to most of these questions, perhaps you could become an eco entrepreneur!

People who set up their own businesses rather than working for other people are called entrepreneurs. An eco entrepreneur runs their business in such a way that it causes the least damage to the environment. Some eco businesses tackle environmental problems while others sell environmentally-friendly goods or services.

The reason that most entrepreneurs put in the hard work to run their own business is in the hope of making money (profit).

Eco entrepreneurs often give away some of their profit to help the environment. They might give to a global organisation, a wildlife charity or a local environmental project. They may even set up the business as a not-for-profit organisation, where all the profits are put back into the business (after paying wages to the people who work for the business).

Recycling, upcycling and downcycling

Our planet has limited resources that we can use to make things. Reusing products that are no longer of use in their original form is an important way to limit the use of raw materials.

Recycling

- Recycling turns waste products into new products of a similar type. The new product has a similar value to the original.

Downcycling

- Downcycling turns waste materials into products of a lesser value. Materials can be downcycled a few times. Each time they become less valuable.

Upcycling

- Upcycling turns waste products into new products with a different purpose. The new products have the same or more value than the original.

To start an upcycling business you need:

- ✓ A supply of materials that have no more use in their original form.
- ✓ A creative idea about how to use the materials to make a desirable product. This is the most important thing. All the hard work you put in could be wasted if no one wants to buy your finished product.
- ✓ Money to pay for all the things you need to get the business started. These are called start-up costs.
- ✓ Customers or consumers: people who will buy the product or service. For your business to make money there must be enough customers who want to buy the products at the price you are charging.
- ✓ A lot of energy and enthusiasm.

Pages 14, 16, 19, 21 and 22 have fictitious examples of four different types of upcycling business with an explanation of how to set them up in order to make a profit.

PRODUCT DESIGN

In most businesses, designers create products and then think about what materials they could use to make them. In an upcycling business, the first stage is to find a supply of unwanted items or materials. Then the designer uses their imagination and their skills to think about how the unwanted items or materials can be upcycled into something more desirable.

Raw materials

One of the advantages of starting an upcycling business is that the raw materials you use to make the product are often free or cost very little. Look around to see if you have a supply of materials you can upcycle into new products.

Upcycling discarded materials could save them from being sent to a landfill site where they would be thrown into a big hole in the ground and covered with soil. Alternatively they might be burned in a large incinerator. Both of these methods of disposal can cause pollution both now and in the future as the components break down in a process that may take thousands of years.

We have a Sunday newspaper every week. The comic strip is very colourful.

You could upcycle it into lots of different paper products.

Starting your own business at an early age can have drawbacks. Opening a bank account and selling through online websites will mean you will need an adult to help you. Do you know anyone who has started their own business? Is there a teacher at your school who is interested in supporting young entrepreneurs? These people may act as your mentors to help you through the process.

The Internet

Look at websites such as Pinterest and Etsy.

Search on Google Images to get ideas for products that can be made from comics or newsprint. Books and magazines are a good source of ideas too.

Product research

Books and magazines

There are a lot of books on upcycling. Have a look in your local library. Magazines such as *Reloved* specialise in upcycling projects.

Try to think of something completely unique, or think of a way to give a twist to an existing product. This will make your product stand out from those already available.

YouTube

There are a lot of tutorials to watch on YouTube to show you how to make paper products step-by-step.

Prototype

Choose two or three different ideas and make some finished products. You will need to repeat this stage a few times to get the finished products right. These sample products are called prototypes.

Use a notebook to make notes on each prototype.

Possible ideas:

✓ **Comic-strip bunting**   Quick to make – and it looks very effective. It uses a lot of magazine paper.

✓ **Woven basket**   This took me too long to make.

✓ **Comic-strip coasters**   Cool!

✓ **Comic-strip lampshade**   This took me seven hours to make but looks great.

✓ **Colour magazine paper beads**   I made 50 beads after school and still had time to do my homework.

THE MARKET

Businesses sell to customers or consumers. A market is anywhere that buyers and sellers meet to exchange goods or services for money. It can be the Internet, a shopping catalogue or the high street. Markets are competitive, with many companies trying to sell similar products to the same group of customers.

Market research

It makes good sense to spend some time finding out about the market for your products before you start to sell them. It could save you time and money in the long run as if the research shows that not many people like them you can start again and think of another idea. This type of research is called market research.

Show your prototypes to as many people as you can. Design a questionnaire with questions about each product. Find people willing to answer your questionnaire and record their answers. Ask a broad range of different people, such as friends, parents, teachers, friends' parents, relatives and neighbours.

Ask people about their shopping habits, their spending habits and what they like and dislike about your products. A few examples are shown on the clipboard opposite but you can make your questionnaire much more detailed if you wish. Think carefully about what information is going to be useful to you when setting up your business. The information you gather is called feedback.

! Do not set off on your own with your questionnaire. Take a parent with you.

Recycled paper products

1   Age 10–20   (21–40)   41–60   over 60

2   How likely are you to buy any of these products? Rate each product from one to ten, with one being 'not very likely to buy it' and ten being 'very likely to buy it'.

Paper bead
necklace   1 2 3 (4) 5 6 7 8 9 10

Lampshade   1 (2) 3 4 5 6 7 8 9 10

Bunting   1 2 3 4 5 6 7 (8) 9 10

Coasters   1 2 3 4 5 6 7 8 (9) 10

3   How much would you spend on each product?

Paper bead
necklace   £4 £5 (£6) £7 £8 £9 £10 more than £10

Lampshade   £7 £8 £9 £10 more than £10

Bunting   £2 £3 £4 £5 (£6) £7 £8 £9 £10 more than £10

Coasters   £3 (£4) £5 £6

4   Where would you buy products like this? Choose one or more of these options.

- ☑ Internet
- ☐ Shop
- ☐ Catalogue
- ☑ Craft fair
- ☐ Market

What does the market research tell you?

When the results of all the questionnaires were collated the most popular products were those made from comic strips. It is most likely they would be purchased by people aged between 20 and 40 from an online shopping site or a craft fair.

Would you buy this?

Yes, it looks great.

MARKETING

Marketing is all the things associated with buying and selling a product and finding customers. When you have identified a market for your products, you can target the marketing to that group.

The four aspects of marketing are product, price, place and promotion. This is called the marketing mix. Getting the right marketing mix is the way to achieve maximum sales.

Product – Create a product that a group of customers want

The things that make your product different from the competition are its Unique Selling Points (USPs). To find out more about USPs see page 12.

Price – Price the product appropriately

Setting the correct price for a product is important for both sales and profit.

- Work out exactly how much a product takes to make. This is called the **unit cost**. If you are making a lot of similar products, work out the unit cost by dividing the cost of the raw materials by the number of products you can make from them.

- The difference between the price you sell each product for (the selling price) and the unit cost is the **profit margin**.

- Look at the market research to see if this is a price that customers might be prepared to pay.

- Look at your competitors to see what they charge. If your products are cheaper or more expensive there needs to be a clear reason why.

Place – Have products on sale somewhere that customers visit

Where will your potential customers be looking for products to buy?

✓ **Market stalls**
The best located stalls, also called pitches, in busy markets are booked a long time in advance.

✓ **Craft fairs**
There will be lots of people selling crafts. The people who attend craft fairs like handmade objects.

✓ **The Internet**
The Internet gives your business access to a global marketplace, 24 hours a day, but there is a lot of competition.

✓ **High-street shops**
Only the people who shop in that area are going to see your products. Shop owners need to make a profit from selling your goods in their shop so they will pay you a wholesale price, which is lower than the selling price (see page 10).

Promotion – Make people aware that your products are for sale

These are ways to make people aware of your products at the right time by promoting them.

Advertising

This is paid for advertising that can be scheduled throughout the year.
- Print advertising in newspapers
- TV advertising
- Social media advertising

Publicity

Publicity is free. It is generated by stunts or events such as charitable donations and new product launches. Not all publicity is good.
- Interviews on TV or radio
- Interviews in magazines and newspapers

Sales promotions

Promotions are paid for. They are designed to increase sales for a short period.
- Money-off coupons
- Flash sales
- Competitions

GREAT DEAL

LIMITED TIME ONLY

BRANDING

Although you may have developed a range of very different products, they are all part of the brand that you are selling. Branding is the image that your company and your products have in the market. When a brand develops the trust of its customers so that they buy the same brand again and again, it is called brand loyalty.

USPs

If you are working with other people, get together and say or write down all the words you can think of that describe the products and the business. This is called brainstorming.

Are there things that make your product more attractive than the competition? These are your Unique Selling Points (USPs).

The USPs of your products can be used to make them stand out from the competition.

Decide on the most important USPs and design a strong brand image to get them across to your customers.

Brand name

A good brand name is memorable.

It might describe what you do, such as:

The Recycled Paper Company

It might make people smile, such as:

zap-pow crafts

It could be based on your name:

Lizzie B

When you have decided on a name you can design a logo for the brand.

What makes a good logo?

✓ It is unique.

✓ The style is appropriate for the target audience.

✓ It works in black and white, grey tone and in colour.

✓ It works large and small.

✓ It works for all the products.

If you are creating a brand selling upcycled products, the core values of the company could be to promote 'green' values. This is your business ethos. A green business ethos may persuade customers to buy the products even if they are more expensive than those of a competitor.

Look at everything about your business and try to apply an eco-friendly policy to everything you do.

- Can the packaging be recycled?

- Is the packaging made from recycled materials?

- How do you transport the products? Carrying them by foot or on your bicycle are the best ways.

- You may wish to be a socially responsible business and support a local wildlife or environment project.

SELLING ON THE INTERNET

Manufacturing businesses sell their products to customers all over the world through online shops. A shop selling products from a website is called an e-commerce site (see page 27).

Selling on an online gallery site

You can set up a shop on these sites to sell vintage, handmade and unusual craft products. The site charges a commission on each sale.

Advantages

✓ All the advertising to draw customers to the site is done for you.

✓ You do not need your own website.

✓ Customers who visit these websites like unusual handmade products.

✓ The sites are easy to use.

✓ A lot of customers visit these sites.

Disadvantages

✗ Some sites charge a joining fee as well as a commission on each sale.

✗ Not everyone can join.

✗ They are specialist sites so there is a lot of competition.

✗ Brand loyalty is with the website rather than with the products.

BUSINESS IDEA 1

www.zap-pow.com Upcycled comic-strip products

The business idea

Using the results of your market research you have decided to make a range of upcycled products from comic strips. You are going to sell them from an online gallery site specialising in handmade and vintage products.

How to sell on an online gallery

Photograph your products

Product shots are really important when selling on the Internet as customers cannot feel the products or see them in real life.

You will need:

✓ A reasonable camera or smartphone
✓ A tripod
✓ A neutral background

A gallery site will have space for a large product shot and some gallery shots (see below) of each product.

Product shot Set up your shot indoors, using natural light from a window. Use a sheet of white card as a background to avoid hard lines. See Further information on page 31 for useful websites to show you how to set this up.

Gallery shots Take a selection of the following:

- Shots to show the scale of each product
- Close-ups of any important details
- Photos of the product from a range of angles
- Lifestyle shots to make the product look desirable

Write about your products

Write a clear description of each product including the size, colour, material it is made from and your USPs (see page 12).

Set up your shop

The gallery site will have step-by-step instructions to help you do this.

When an item sells, you will be notified by email. The payment will go straight into your bank or you can set up an account with an online payment service such as PayPal and have the money transferred into that.

Post out the items directly to the customer.

HOW TO SELL AT A CRAFT FAIR

A craft fair is a good place to sell handmade upcycled items. Look in the local press and online to see what fairs are in your area.

BUSINESS IDEA 2

Upsa Daisy Upcycled garden products

The business idea

To make a range of upcycled products for the garden such as: cutlery wind chimes, tin-can planters, jam-jar candle holders and spoon plant labels. To sell the products at a craft fair.

What to do:

Design and make the products to sell. Make a range of products – some of them expensive and others inexpensive.

Create a natural, upcycled brand image

- Recycled card labels
- Natural string to tie on labels
- A hand-drawn sign on a children's blackboard for your brand name.

Research

- Work out exactly how much each product costs to make and then add a profit margin (see page 10).
- Look at your competitors' products to see what they charge.
- Look at the price of similar products on Internet selling sites.
- Products at craft fairs are usually a little cheaper than those selling in the shops as you are selling direct to the customer and don't have to pay commission.

Decide what type of craft fair would be the best market for your products. There are many different types.

✓ **Small local fairs**
These work well in tourist areas if your products have a local connection. Do you use local wool or fabric, or use any local or traditional skills to make the product?

✓ **Specialist fairs**
Vintage, gift fairs or Christmas fairs.

✓ **Craft markets**
There is often a waiting list for stalls in popular craft markets.

✓ **County shows**
It is often quite expensive to book a stall at a county show, and bookings are made a long way ahead. If you know an adult who has booked a stand, perhaps they would let you take a few pieces to sell in exchange for helping them sell their products.

✓ **School fairs**
These are ideal places to show your products for the first time in order to see if people like them.

Once you have decided which type of fair would suit your products best:
- Book a stall. Ask if you need to take out insurance.
- Make lots of products to sell. This is called your stock.
- Decide on prices. Make price labels.
- Make printed or handmade business cards to hand out on the day.

Things to take on the day:
- Cash box and plenty of coins of different values (your float).
- Things to dress the table: tablecloths or lengths of printed fabric; baskets for different products; garden flowers in vintage jugs.
- If you are outside, be prepared for any type of weather. A plastic sheet is useful to cover up your products if it rains and a huge umbrella will help to keep you dry.

AN UPCYCLING BLOG OR VLOG

Are you creative?

Do you get bored making the same things over and over again?

If the answer to these questions is 'yes' then an upcycling blog or vlog might be the business for you.

Many people visit websites to find out how to do and make things. If you have a skill such as upcycling you could turn your knowledge into a successful Internet blog or vlog. To find out more about blogs and vlogs, and setting up a website, see page 27.

To set up a blog or vlog you will need:

✓ A reasonable camera or smartphone.

✓ A blog site. Some blog sites, such as WordPress and Tumblr, can be set up for free. Log in and follow the instructions to create a domain name (see page 27) and design your site. If you want a vlog site then go to YouTube.com and create a channel for your videos.

✓ Somewhere to work.

✓ Raw materials and discarded items to upcycle into new products to sell.

✓ Some fantastic ideas for upcycling projects.

To set up a vlog site you will also need:

✓ A reasonable video camera, and either someone to operate it or a tripod. It is difficult to glue and sew while operating a video camera or phone!

BUSINESS IDEA 3

Lizzie-B Craft workshop channel

The business idea

To set up a blog and vlog to show people how to upcycle unwanted clothes or other objects and make them into beautiful and useful items.

What to do:

✓ Make videos showing how to upcycle a product step-by-step. Keep the videos short and leave a gap between stages so that viewers can pause the video as they make the product.

✓ Take photos of the finished item to post on the site.

✓ Upload the videos to your YouTube channel.

✓ Upload the written content and photos to your blog site.

✓ Link to Facebook, Twitter and Instagram. Tweet about your blog. Send photos via Instagram. Sign up to Google Analytics. Update your Facebook page regularly about what you are doing and keep adding content to the site.

How to make money from the site:

• Contact craft suppliers to see if they would be interested in paying to put a link on the site.

• Apply for Google AdSense. If you are accepted, advertisers will bid to put adverts on your site and you will be paid every time someone clicks on one of them. To be accepted, you need interesting information on your blog.

Blogs and vlogs are easy and cheap to set up but it can take a long time to start earning money from them.

Be very careful about what you say on social media. Do not do or say anything that you may regret later.

PRODUCTION

The production process is all the things you do to materials to make them into products.

Types of production process

Mass production

When a lot of identical products are made in a factory, usually on an assembly line, they are described as mass-produced. These products are available to buy in lots of different outlets on the high street and online. The only difference is the price. Customers can compare prices and choose where to buy.

One-off products

When products are made one at a time they are one-offs. Because they are unique the price cannot be compared. Customers may be prepared to pay a high price for a one-off item that no one else owns.

Limited edition products

When a limited number of a particular product are produced they are limited edition products. The product is sold as part of a numbered batch.

Limiting the number of a product can add value.

Bespoke production

Bespoke products are specially made for a customer to suit their needs. They are handmade, usually by skilled artists or craftspeople. The price is agreed between the customer and the maker.

Personalised products

Personalised products are made unique by adding an individual's name, initials or other symbol.

BUSINESS IDEA 4

Vintage Vogue Upcycled costume jewellery

 You have made a few pieces of jewellery out of broken beads and necklaces. When you wear them people comment on how lovely they are.

The business idea

To make a few pieces of unique jewellery to sell at a high price. Customers are often keen to buy something that cannot be bought anywhere else.

What you will need:

✓ Glue, jewellery fastenings, mini glue gun and other jewellery-making equipment.

✓ A supply of broken jewellery. Charity shops are a good place to buy broken jewellery at a reasonable cost. If you are lucky, the charity shop might give you any broken jewellery that cannot be re-sold.

Now make some spectacular pieces of jewellery. Take great care to make them properly. Quality is very important for one-off pieces.

Decide how to sell them.

✓ **In retail shops or galleries**
If they are beautiful items of jewellery, try bridal shops.
Brides often look for something unique to accessorise to their dress.

✓ **Local art and craft galleries**
Galleries often use display cabinets for one-off items. They take a commission when items sell, which means that you only get some of the value of the sale. Craft fairs are another option.

✓ **Vintage markets**
Markets specialising in high quality retro and old items.

✓ **Online**
See pages 14–15 for advice on how to do this.

INVENTIONS

Do you have a completely new idea about how to upcycle products or materials that have reached the end of their useful life? If your idea is completely new it is an invention. Turning an invention into a product and marketing it is called innovation.

BUSINESS IDEA 5

Your very own upcycling invention

The business idea

To turn a product that you have invented into a profitable eco business.

How to protect your idea

You can't. An idea is in your head and it is just the first step towards an invention. To protect your idea you will need to write it down in detail. Once an idea has enough detail that you can explain it to others it becomes an invention and at that stage you can apply for a patent to stop other people copying it.

To apply for a patent you will need:

- ✓ A detailed description of how the invention works.
- ✓ A prototype – if this is not possible, make sketches and drawings.
- ✓ Details of how the invention is different from anything else on the market.

Funding

Turning an invention into a product and a profitable business is an expensive process. You will need money to do it successfully.

Assets are money or things that you already have that can be sold to raise money.

- Do you have any savings that you could use to start your business?
- Can you earn some money doing odd jobs for family and friends?
- Do you have any old toys, electronic devices or hardly worn clothes that you no longer want? If so, you could sell them – but ask permission first.

Gifts

Family and friends may be prepared to give you money to start your business.

Loans

Family or friends may lend you money to start a business. If they do, make it clear to them that there are risks. If the business does not work out, you will not be able to pay back the loan.

Crowdfunding

This is a relatively new way of raising money for new and innovative products. It raises small amounts of money from a lot of people in exchange for a small reward or stake in the business. You will not be able to get crowdfunding without the help of a mentor (see page 6).

What to do:

✓ Create a page on a crowdfunding website. Include a short video, photographs and information about the invention.

✓ Share the website with as many people as you can.

✓ Offer a reward for those who donate. These can be related to the size of the donation. There are suggestions on the websites.

PEOPLE, PLANET, PROFIT

A business plan is everything about your business written down in one place. It is given to people or organisations, such as banks, when businesses need to raise money to start or invest in a business.

For

✓ It is a good way to make sure that you have thought of everything.

✓ You can show it to a possible mentor to explain what you want to do.

Against

✗ A traditional business plan looks at what the business will be doing in five years time but small businesses today are moving and changing quickly.

✗ Sitting at your desk writing a complicated plan can waste precious time when you could be getting customer feedback and real-life experience.

Pitching your idea

If you are looking for a sponsor or are selling the business idea to a mentor or a teacher at school, you will need to give them a summary of the business. This is known as a pitch. A pitch is a short presentation summarising your business idea and answering questions about it. This may seem scary, but as an entrepreneur you will need to learn to sell ideas so now is a good time to start.

An eco business plan highlights not only how your business will make a profit but the environmental and social benefits of the business.

✓ Explain how the business helps to save resources.

✓ Explain how the business is environmentally friendly.

✓ Practise in front of a mirror or practise giving your presentation to a friend.

I hope they like the idea.

The figures look impressive.

A BUSINESS PLAN

Summary

The first part of a business plan is a summary. That sounds odd because a summary is usually at the end, but it is placed at the front so that the person reading it can understand the business from the beginning. Write it last as by then you will have all the information you need.

The business idea

Describe what you intend to sell.
Describe the environmental and social impact of the idea.
How are you going to ensure that your business has a positive or a neutral impact on the environment?

Objectives

Why do you want a business? What would you like the business to achieve in the short term and the long term? Are you planning to give back to the community in any way?

About you

What have you done that will help you to set up and run a business?

Finance

Information about costing and pricing your products or services. The amount of money you need to set up the business and run it until you begin to get money back into the business from customers.

The market

Describe the customers who will buy your products or services. Describe the competition you will face.

Market research

What market research have you done? See pages 8 and 9.

Why will you succeed when lots of businesses fail?

In two columns write a list of your:
Strengths, weaknesses, opportunities and threats.

This is called a **SWOT** analysis.

RUNNING YOUR BUSINESS

There are tasks that need to be done every day to keep a business running smoothly.

Every day

✓ Manage social media accounts – keep in touch with other businesses and with potential customers.

    ✓ Send out orders.

    ✓ Make up stock.

    ✓ Think up new ideas.

    ✓ Check the money going into and out of the bank account (cash flow).

Things to be aware of:

✓ The possibility of expanding your business into different areas.

✓ The need to increase prices if raw materials become more expensive.

✓ The idea of increasing your product range. Constantly adding new products to an Internet site means that your business will appear higher in the Google search ratings.

✓ Diversifying into a new type of product.

✓ Boosting sales with a promotional event or special offer.

Giving back

If your business is profitable this is the time to think about ways to give back to the community.

- Choose a charity to donate to when customers make a purchase. If the charity has a connection to your product, so much the better.

- If you have funded your business through a crowdfunding site, perhaps you could choose another business to help.

SETTING UP A WEBSITE

There are a lot of different types of websites.
These are the ones most commonly used.

Blog websites

These are interactive sites where both you and those who follow you can post messages. They link easily with all other social media platforms (Twitter, Instagram, Facebook), which makes them perfect for lifestyle websites.

Vlog websites

These sites are similar to blogs but are video-based and placed on video channels such as YouTube and Vimeo. This makes them ideal for music showcase websites.

e-commerce sites

If you want to sell directly from the website you will need an e-commerce site. This type of site is linked to a merchant system that deals with checkout payments and refunds. A merchant system is run by a bank or credit card processing organisation such as PayPal. These secure systems are separate from your website so you do not have to worry about protecting customers' bank account details. They also check a customers' bank account to make sure there are enough funds so you do not need to worry about getting paid.

Buy a domain name

Check that the brand name you have chosen is available as a domain name. You can do this on any of the domain selling sites such as Go-Daddy. There are many different versions of website names, with 'forsale.com' and 'forsale.co.uk' being the most memorable. If the name you want is for sale you can buy it online for one or more years. You will be emailed when it is due for renewal.

Web hosting

Once you have a domain name address you need to put it onto the Internet. Web hosting companies rent you a space on their computer system (web server). The domain address means that search engines can find you on the internet in much the same way as people find your address to send a letter. Web hosting companies charge a monthly fee. Some web design packages will host your site for free as well but take care. These free sites may have restrictions about how you can make money from your website, so in the long run it may be better to pay the fee.

Web design

There are free design tools to help you do this. Usually there are a range of template designs available that can be customised to your liking. Many come with videos to show you how to set them up step-by-step.

NOW WHAT?

✓ You have a successful business

Running a business is exciting as things are always changing, especially for eco entrepreneurs who are always looking for new ways to reduce the negative effects of existing products on the environment. Fashions change, customers needs change and you will need to be flexible to stay ahead of the competition.

Problems and solutions

Your supply of raw materials dries up.

Have two or three different sources of raw materials so that if one source dries up you can still carry on selling.

Your outlet closes.
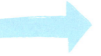
Choose at least two ways of selling your products or have two different products for sale in two outlets. That way, if one is not successful or closes you can continue to sell.

A competitor starts to sell a very similar product.

Add new products to your range – the ones you (hopefully) have been developing whilst selling the first ones. If your brand image is strong and your customers are loyal they may still prefer to buy your products.

Opportunities

Always be on the lookout for new sources of raw materials to upcycle.

Learn all you can about how different products harm the environment and see if you can think of a green alternative.

✗ Your business is not making money

You have tried your best but your business is not making money. What should you do?

Try to work out what went wrong

You will have learned a lot by starting up a business. Do you know why your business idea did not work?

Go to page 10 and look at the marketing mix. Look at the products, pricing, places you were selling and your methods of promotion and see if you can identify a problem.

What next?

The great thing about running your own business is that you can decide its future.

An eco entrepreneur is not only inspired by profit but also by their passion for creating a better environment. If your business has been profitable but you have a better idea you can use everything you have learned setting up the first business to be even more successful next time.

If you were not successful go back to the beginning and start again. If being an eco entrepreneur is your passion, failure will not put you off. Very few successful entrepreneurs achieve success with the first business they set up. Running a business that you care about is worth the effort.

"I'M CONVINCED THAT ABOUT HALF OF WHAT SEPARATES THE SUCCESSFUL ENTREPRENEURS FROM THE NON-SUCCESSFUL ONES IS PURE PERSEVERANCE."

Steve Jobs, founder of Apple (1955–2011)

BUSINESS JARGON

A glossary of business words and expressions

A

advertising Activities, such as displaying posters, placing adverts or broadcasting adverts on TV, that attract attention to products or services.

assets In business, money, property or things of value that are owned by the business.

B

blog A website set up to encourage and interact with its followers, or an article posted on a website.

brainstorming A way of coming up with creative solutions by encouraging people to suggest everything they can think of, however improbable.

brand The type of product produced by a company or the image that a business has created of itself (of quality, low-cost, luxury etc).

business An organisation that makes goods or provides services, and sells them for money.

business plan A report that includes all the research about a business idea, including how it aims to make money.

C

commission A payment made to the seller of goods when products are sold.

company Any type of business that trades goods or services.

consumer In business, the person who buys a product or service.

customer Someone who buys products or services.

E

eco Not harming the natural environment.

eco entrepreneur An entrepreneur who makes environmentally-friendly products and runs a business with as little negative impact on the environment as possible.

e-commerce (electronic commerce) Buying and selling over the Internet.

entrepreneur Someone who starts a business, taking on the responsibility for the risks and rewards.

environment The natural world.

ethical Here, keeping to a set of goals that avoid actions that might bring harm to the natural world.

F

feedback A customer's reactions to a product or service, which can be used to improve the performance of a business.

G

goods A physical product, such as a cake or a car, that can be sold to supply a want or a need.

green Here, products or services that do not harm the natural environment.

L

legislation Laws passed by a government.

loan Money lent from one person or organisation to another.

logo A recognisable symbol or name for a company.

loyalty In business, when customers buy again.

M

market A place where goods or services are traded for money, such as a shop, stall or website.

market research Gathering information about the market for a product or service.

marketing All the activities needed to sell a product or service, including advertising, promotion and sales.

mentor A person with experience who acts as an advisor to someone with less experience.

P

pitch A presentation summarising a business idea. Also, a place to set up a market stall.

product An item that has been manufactured for sale.

production The process of making a product.

profit The amount of money left over once costs have been deducted from sales.

promotion Ways of letting people know that your business and products exist.

prototype A sample of a product made for research purposes, which will be changed and tweaked before manufacturing the final product.

Q

questionnaire A list of questions used to collect information about a specific subject, product or service.

R

raw materials The materials used to make a product.

recycle To reuse products or materials.

research To find out more information about something.

resources Here refers to natural resources, such as water, forests, fertile land and minerals (coal, oil, tin, wool, paper etc).

S

services Activities such as banking or hairdressing that can be sold to customers.

social media Websites or apps (applications) that enable people to communicate by creating and sharing content over the Internet.

socially responsible A person or organisation that is concerned with helping the local community or local environment while also making a profit.

start-up A new business set up for the first time.

start-up costs The one-off costs of starting a new business.

stock The goods or products that are ready to sell (stored in a shop or warehouse).

U

unit cost The cost of making a single product.

USPs (Unique Selling Points) The things that make a company or a product stand out from its competitors.

V

vintage Something from the past that has a value.

vlog A video blog.

Further information

https://www.shopify.co.uk/blog/12206313-the-ultimate-diy-guide-to-beautiful-product-photography
A step-by-step guide to taking great product shots.

http://thewhoot.com.au/whoot-news/crafty-corner/upcycled-jeans-skirt
There are many different upcycling projects on the Internet including this one. If you are good with a sewing machine and have an old pair of jeans this might be a fun upcycling project.

http://sustainablog.org/2014/02/upcycled-t-shirt-rosettes/
If you have an old T-shirt that you no longer want you could try making it into scarves.

http://www.fabartdiy.com/fabartdiy-pallet-home-decorating-and-furniture-projects-and-tutorials/
Use this website to help you turn old wooden pallets into great pieces of furniture.

Books

Be creative: Customise your clothes by Anna Claybourne (Franklin Watts, 2015)

Craft Attack! Recycling Crafts by Annalees Lim (Franklin Watts, 2014)

Note to parents and teachers: every effort has been made by the Publishers to ensure that these websites are suitable for children, that they are of the highest educational value, and that they contain no inappropriate or offensive material.
However, because of the nature of the Internet, it is impossible to guarantee that the contents of these sites will not be altered.
We strongly advise that Internet access is supervised by a responsible adult.

INDEX

advertising 11, 14, 19
analysis, SWOT 25
assets 23

blogs 18–19, 27
brainstorming 12
branding 12–13, 14, 16, 27, 28
business, closing down a 29
business plan, developing a 24–25

cost, unit 10, 16
costs, start-up 5, 25
crowdfunding 23, 26

downcycling 5

e-commerce 6, 9, 11, 14–15, 16, 21, 26–27
ethos, business 13

fairs, craft 9, 11, 16–17, 21
finance, start-up 23

ideas, business
    Lizzie B craft workshop channel 13, 19
    upcycled invention 22–23
    Upsa Daisy upcycled garden products
        16–17
    Vintage Vogue upcycled vintage
        jewellery 21
    zap-pow upcycled comic-strip products 6,
        7, 9, 13, 14–15
inventions 22–23

loans 23
logos 13

marketing mix 10–11, 22, 29
materials, raw 5, 6, 10, 18, 20, 22, 26, 28
mentors 6, 23, 24
monetise, ways to 19

organisation, not-for-profit 4

packaging 13
patents 22
photography 15
pitch, preparing a 24

pricing 10–11, 16, 17, 20, 25, 29
product range 26, 28
production process 20–21
profit margin 10, 16
promotion 11, 26, 29
prototypes 7, 8, 22
publicity 11

questionnaires 8–9

recycling 5
research
    market 8–10, 14, 16, 25
    product 6–7

sites, online gallery 14–15, 16, 19, 21, 27
social media, using 11, 18, 19, 23, 26–27

USPs (Unique Selling Points) 10, 12, 15

vlogs 18–19, 27

YouTube 7, 18, 19, 27

These are the list of contents for each title in the How to make money series.

How to make money from cooking and baking

Why start a business? · Finding a business idea · Finding the right product · Try things out · The right price · A healthy image · Planning · Money, money, money · Making the snacks · Cooking blogs and vlogs · Baking for money · Baking for charity · Have you thought of this? · Promotion

How to make money from your computer

Why start a business? · Selling on the Internet · Create a brand · Blogs and vlogs · Review blogs · Showcase your talent · Crazy stuff · Ways to monetise · Making money from apps or games · Money, money, money · Selling computer services

How to make money from upcycling

Why start a business? · Product design · The market · Marketing · Branding · Selling on the Internet · How to sell at a craft fair · An upcycling blog or vlog · Production · Inventions · People, planet, profit · Running your business · Setting up a website

How to make money from your spare time

Why start a business? · The idea · Research · Target marketing · Creating a brand · Pricing · Production · Selling · The Internet · Use your skills · Offer a service · Get SMART · Work part-time